Lord with a Hood

Volume 1

Arthur Steers

ISBN 979-8-89485-111-2 (Paperback)
ISBN 979-8-89485-112-9 (Digital)

Covenant Books
11661 Hwy 707
Murrells Inlet, SC 29576
www.covenantbooks.com

Episode 1

Lift Your Eyes

"Today is going to be a good day!" I said out loud. My normal routine was full of praise, prayer, spreading the good news of Jesus, and reading the Bible. I did that every day.

Later that night, I got home from work, went to bed, and had a dream. In the dream, I saw pillars of white and was in a throne room of some sort. On the throne, I saw Jesus.

He said, "Come here, my child, I have a gift for you." I saw him create a black hood with a chain out of nowhere! Then he said to me, "Put it on. There are things coming that you won't understand. I choose you to help protect." So I put it on.

After that, I woke up and realized the hood in the dream was on me! Then I heard God's voice say, "I choose you, Alexander Peterson, because of a world threat. Satan is going to give someone powers, so I did the same for you. There are also swords on the desk. Let me show you how to use your powers in the backyard."

"Okay, God!"

*****

"Ah, evil is not bad, just something more!"
"You are so right!"
"Who was that?"

"The one you follow. Satan. And I got a job for you, plus a gift. It's a hood with red and black. Put it on and use its power! There are dark swords too. Start big, and go rob the bank. Go!"

*****

"What should you call me, God?" I asked.
God said, "You will be called Lord with a Hood."
"Why is it black though?"
"It is a symbol that you're a sinner still, and I choose you. It's time, Lord with a Hood. There is someone already Satan picked. He's at the bank, robbing it. Lord with a Hood, remember, you can't win every battle, but you can win the war."

*****

"Ha ha ha, all of it is mine. No one can stop me!"
"Are you sure about that?"
"Who are you?"
"Lord with a Hood, and you're putting that money all back."
"We'll see about that!" He ran at me with his swords, and I blocked it using mine.

I used my force powers to push him back, and he hit a wall. He dropped the bag of money when he hit the wall. He got up and raised his sword. When he did that, three black lightning bolts hit the ground in front of him, and three black figures appeared. Evil Lord with a Hood ran, and they came after me. I used my electric powers and hit the middle Dark Minion, causing a chain reaction that destroyed the others as well. I went over to where the money bag was and gave it back to the banker. Then the people started thanking me. I told them it wasn't me they should be thanking; it was God. He was the one who gave me these abilities. If it wasn't for him, it would have been worse. Then they started thanking God, and I left.

When I got home, I heard God's voice again. He told me there was a lot more coming, and he'd let me know when it was time. He said if I ever need anything, he would be with me.

I lift up my eyes to the hills. From where does my help come? My help comes from the Lord, who made heaven and earth. (Psalm 121:1–2)

Nothing Is Impossible

I'd been training with my new powers and weapons for a week now. I found out I had speed powers too! Evil Lord with a Hood had not done anything since the bank he tried to rob. As I waited for God to give me a sign that I was needed again, I'd been reading the Bible and listening to Christian music on the radio. I decided to do something for a change. I had an idea! I finally knew how to use my speed, so I used it to run up the Saint Louis arch and sit on top, waiting for something back from God.

*****

"Evil Lord with a Hood, I have a plan to stop him. Destroy the stadium and everyone in it!"

"As you wish, Satan."

*****

"Hey! This is a restricted area. There's a game on the field!"

"I know that. Move!"

"No!"

"Well, I'll make you then. Ahhh! Those are dark chains, not breaking those anytime soon. Dark Minions, clear the field!"

They responded, "Yes, Evil Lord with a Hood!"

"Give me the microphone!"

"Okay."

"Well, the stadium of Saint Louis City, you all have a surprise I cooked up for all of you today! Now I'm Evil Lord with a Hood, and the show is about to begin! Ha ha ha ha!"

*****

"Lord with a Hood, it's time. Evil Lord with a Hood is at the baseball stadium."

"Okay, on it!"

"One more thing—he's trying to get you, so it's a trap. Be careful and remember the main priority is keeping everyone safe."

"Okay."

"Hurry!"

I ran with my speed powers to get there. When I got there, there were Dark Minions at all the entrances. So I used my electric powers to cause a chain reaction like last time, and it worked. When I reached the field door, I saw Evil Lord with a Hood with a little black ball. It looked like it was sucking things in and getting bigger. I realized it was a black hole he made.

Then I heard him say, "Lord with a Hood, if you are smart, you would surrender."

So without him noticing, I got all the people out using my speed powers.

After I had taken out all of them, Evil Lord with a Hood realized they were all gone and said, "I know it's you, Lord with a Hood! Even though you got them out, it doesn't mean you can stop a black hole."

"Yes, Evil Lord with a Hood, I can't, but you underestimate God! You follow Satan. I follow God! Nothing is impossible with him!" So I used my electric powers and created a barrier of electricity around the black hole. I used my speed powers to run around it, making it smaller and smaller until it was nothing again.

"That's impossible!" said Evil Lord with a Hood.

"Nothing is impossible with God!" I replied.

"I will get you, Lord with a Hood, if it's the last thing I'll do! Minions, attack!" He ran away after they started running at me. I used my force powers and pushed them back, and they ran too.

After they ran, I checked to see if everyone was okay. Then the people started thanking me. I told them, "Jesus is the way. If it wasn't for him, I wouldn't be protecting you, so don't thank me, thank him." Then, like a crowd at the stadium, they started praising God. So I left and went back home.

> But Jesus looked at them and said, "With man this is impossible, but with God all things are possible." (Matthew 19:26)

Episode 3

Truth and Lies

It had been four days since the stadium incident with Evil Lord with a Hood. Since then, I've been in Saint Charles by the Missouri River, admiring God's creation. I had to admit, getting used to all these abilities and all that's going on is not easy. I couldn't even get why God chose me for this job, but he did. Now I'm just waiting for when I'm needed again.

*****

"I can't believe this! He stopped our plan!"

"Yes, he did, and I got a better one to stop him! Go to the Saint Charles Courthouse and play desperate to convince them you're good and he's bad. He won't stand a chance!"

"That's the best plan yet! Ha ha ha ha!"

*****

"Officers! I need help! There's someone in a black hood, and he wants to kill me!"

"Sir, what did he look like?"

"I don't know. All I saw was his hood, and he came at me. I need a dispatch right away."

*****

"Lord with a Hood, it is time. Go to the courthouse."
"Okay!"
"There is a thing you need to know. Being a protector does not always mean using your powers. Sometimes the only way to win is to lay your weapons down."
"Okay!"
I used my speed powers to get there. When I did, there was a whole police squad. So I stopped and put down my swords. Then a cop came to me and said, "You have the right to remain silent." Then he cuffed me and took me to a holding cell.
I waited and heard God's voice again. He said that this was not permanent and I had to be patient. So I waited.

*****

"Thanks for your help, officers."
"Just doing my job."

*****

"Ah, I can do anything I want now. Lord with a Hood is finally gone! I'll rob the bank like I did before he stopped me, and I'll be rich! Ha ha ha ha ha!"

*****

"People, give me all you have and all the money at this bank!"
"Yes, sir."

*****

I overheard on an officer's walkie-talkie that there was a robbery at one of the banks, and they needed officers immediately. So I told him that God was with him, and he would know what to do when it was time. He walked out and said nothing.

*****

"Ah, officers brave enough to face me? Let's test your bravery."

"Is that the guy at the courthouse saying someone was trying to kill him?"

"It seems so, but he has powers of some sort."

"How are we going to stop someone like that?"

"I don't know."

"Hey, do you hear that?"

"Hear what?"

"A voice?"

"No."

"I just had a feeling that we need the guy in the black hood. Right now, we need more than just what we have."

"Sheriff, to the police station. We need the black-hooded person in the cell."

"Okay."

*****

"Black Hood, I don't know why they need you, but all I know is you let yourself get arrested. Why?"

"I have faith in God. The only way to win sometimes is to lay our weapons down."

"I've seen things in my life, but not someone willing to be arrested. So I trust you."

"Don't trust me. Have faith in Jesus."

"Thank you, Black Hood."

"One more thing, it's Lord with a Hood."

"Okay, go get him!"

*****

"Did you release him?"
"Yes, and he's coming in fast. Real fast!"

*****

"Officers, let me handle this. Hey, Evil Lord with a Hood, you know it is against the Ten Commandments to steal."

"Huh? Impossible! How did you get out of that cell?"

"Sometimes, the only way to win is to lay your weapons down, so I let myself get arrested. I had faith in God even though you lied about me. When you started to rob the bank, they saw it was a lie. So they trusted what God told them and let me out. A lie will fail, but the truth stands firm and will not move. I stand for the truth of God. You follow the lies of Satan."

"No! I had enough of this! Dark Minions, attack!"

I used my force powers and pushed them, and they landed on him. Somehow, he started to absorb their power, and he started shooting black fireballs at me. I blocked them with my sword.

Then he said, "This is not the last you heard of me," and vanished.

The officers came over to me and apologized for arresting me. I told them that it was all part of God's plan and that a lie will fail if the truth is firm. They radioed all officers to go and celebrate for God.

I went back home and heard God's voice say, "Today was hard, but there is more to come. When it does, I'll be ready!"

> So Jesus said to the Jews who had believed
> in him, "If you abide in my word, you are truly
> my disciples, and you will know the truth, and
> the truth will set you free." (John 8:31–32)

A Symbol of the Light

It had been a week and four days since Evil Lord with a Hood tried to trick the officers. I had been focusing on the idea of why light is important. For one, you can't see in pitch-black, and the light helps us see. The thing is, though, it's critical for all life. If we had no light, there would be nothing. Even though there are lights in buildings and houses, it's a reminder of where the true light comes from. Jesus is the Light, and he will lead us by his light! So I had been helping people see the true light of Jesus by doing whatever I could to help!

*****

"I have an idea to stop Lord with a Hood in his tracks. He stands for God, so I will destroy the churches so he feels hopeless! Ha ha ha ha!"

*****

"Good morning. I haven't seen you here before."
"I'm new to this area. He he."
"All are welcome, so come inside!"
"Thanks! Ah, it's a shame this place is going to be destroyed. Okay, everyone! I'm here to show you true power! Dark Minions, clear this area so I can make a black hole."

Then a man said to him, "There is no power greater than God's, not even yours!"

Then the whole church agreed and said, "Aman!"

*****

"Lord with a Hood, he is at a church in Maryland Heights. He has a black hole like at the stadium. You know what to do."

"Okay, on it!" So I ran there using my speed.

When I got there, there were two minions at the entrance. I ran between them and used my force powers. They flew in opposite directions and landed on the ground. I went in, and he was in the lobby with the black hole.

I said to him, "Evil Lord with a Hood, what is worth more than Jesus? He is the Way, the Truth, and the Light! Why lose your soul for things less than him and eternity?"

"Because I want what I want, and I will have it all! Satan has what I want. God has nothing I want!"

"Then you made your choice. I've made mine with God."

Evil Lord with a Hood answered, "Then you'll die!"

He ran at me with his swords, and I blocked them. After I blocked those, four of his minions rushed in, so I used my electric powers. I tapped my shoe on the floor, and the electricity spread outward, causing them to fall. By the time I did that, Evil Lord with a Hood was gone again.

Then the church people came up to me and asked if I was a follower of Jesus Christ. I told them yes and that he was the one who gave me these abilities. Then they resumed the service. I sat and listened to the preacher. After it was over, I left and went back home, still amazed at how lights are a reflection of him!

> Again Jesus spoke to them, saying, "I am
> the light of the world. Whoever follows me will
> not walk in darkness, but will have the light of
> life." (John 8:12)

Hope Undeniable

As five days passed, there was no sign of Evil Lord with a Hood. While I waited for God to give me a sign, I was helping churches in the area. Also, I was thinking about the idea of hope. Hope is something everyone needs, and Jesus is our living hope when we trust him.

*****

"This can't be happening! How have my plans all failed! I'm doing this my own way! Dark Minions, we're going to advanced technology to destroy the future, and no one will stand in my way!"

*****

"Hey, this is a restricted area! Now, who gives you these orders? It wasn't me, then it's not important. Stay where you are!"

"Or what?"

"I'll shoot!" *Crunch!*

"It looks like you won't use that anytime soon. Now move! Ah, this lab will be a good place for my black hole, and no one is going to stop me! Minions, clear the floor! I want no one getting in!"

*****

"Lord with a Hood, it's time. He's at the advanced technology center."

"Okay, God, on it! Show them I'm the living hope."

When I got there, there were minions everywhere. So I went in the front entrance. I used my electric powers and force powers to push the electricity, clearing them out on each level. I found Evil Lord with a Hood in the Advanced Weapons Lab and said, "Evil Lord with a Hood, why do you hope for the wrong reason? You hope to gain something of the world, but I hope to gain nothing of it. There is hope for the world with God, but there's nothing but chaos and fear with Satan."

"I choose this because I will be chaos and destruction! I don't care about hope, only me!"

Then he started running at me. I dodged him, and he went into the glass of a gun display. He grabbed the gun and turned it into a gun of his creation. I got my swords out, and he shot at me, but I blocked those shots. He came running at me and pushed me out the window with him. Then he said, "I will see you when you hit the concrete." He used his teleportation powers and vanished. I decided to use my force powers to push myself from the ground and slowly bring me down.

After my feet touched the ground, people ran up to me and said, "This science is more advanced than anything we've seen!"

I said, "This is not science. This is a gift I got from God. Science is what people don't understand about the world, but if we have hope and faith in God that understands all, what more do we need?" Then they started praying to understand more of who he is and started praising him! So I went back home and prayed for people to have more hope in Jesus.

> Blessed be the God and Father of our Lord Jesus Christ! According to his great mercy, he has caused us to be born again to a living hope through the resurrection of Jesus Christ from the dead, to an inheritance that is imperishable, undefiled, and unfading, kept in heaven for you. (1 Peter 1:3–4)

Firm Foundation

It had been four days since Evil Lord with a Hood broke into the Advanced Technology Center. I had been focusing my attention more on God. It is easy to believe in him, but it is hard for all of us to put all our faith, hope, and trust in him. The base is the easy part of a building, but the walls are the hard part. Believing is the easy part. Building it stronger is the hard part. I hoped that when God needed me, I would be ready.

*****

"This is getting old! I want him to be destroyed like he destroyed my plans! I got an idea that will destroy him once and for all! Lord with a Hood will be destroyed tonight! Tonight, we will set a trap at a construction site! Dark Minions, set a trap for him."

*****

"Hey! This is a restricted area!"

"Who restricted it? I have no restrictions because I am Evil Lord with a Hood! So *you* need restrictions!"

"Ahhh!"

"Those are dark chains that cannot be broken! Ah, the cage. When he gets here, he'll be trapped and powerless! Now let's set the black hole up."

*****

"Lord with a Hood, it's time. He's at the construction site by the Mississippi River."

"Okay, on it!"

"One thing—there is a trap, so he is waiting."

I ran there using my speed powers. When I got there, the minions were surrounding the area. I realized there were metal bars, so I used my electric powers to electrify the metal. I found the trap he made and moved it using my speed powers. He didn't notice I moved it.

Then he said, "Lord with a Hood, you have fallen into my trap!"

"You mean this trap?"

"Huh? There's no way you have the trap."

"God always makes a way."

"You have stopped my trap, but you can't stop this black hole! This black hole is the biggest one I made. Have fun trying to stop it! Ha ha ha!"

I did what I did at the stadium. I made a force field and used my speed powers. It got smaller and smaller until it was nothing again.

Then the people ran to the construction site. "The whole construction is gone!"

I came over to them and said, "A weak foundation will be destroyed, but one who builds a strong foundation can withstand a lot more. If Jesus is our firm foundation, nothing can stand against us!"

They started praying for a better foundation with him. I went home and prayed for the same, then went to bed.

> Everyone then who hears these words of
> mine and does them will be like a wise man who
> built his house on the rock. And the rain fell, and
> the floods came, and the winds blew and beat

on that house, but it did not fall because it had been founded on the rock. And everyone who hears these words of mine and does not do them will be like a foolish man who built his house on the sand. And the rain fell, and the floods came, and the winds blew and beat against that house, and it fell, and great was the fall of it. (Matthew 7:24–27)

Jesus Is My Strength

It had been a week since Evil Lord with a Hood tried to trap me at the construction site, and I just found out I had strength powers. But true strength was not about what you can do. True strength came from God. No one had true strength alone. God gives us the strength to walk through any situation. Sometimes, though with strength, you still had to pick up the weights, but he will never leave. He gives us a lot more than we can ever repay, and he gives it for free! All he asks is you trust him. He will always hold you close no matter what! So I'd been showing people that true strength comes from God!

*****

"I'm running out of ideas to end Lord with a Hood!"

"Ah, now you want my help. You should have just said so! There, you have the full extent of your powers. Show the city where power really comes from!"

"As you wish."

"Go tear the city apart!"

"Now that is better planning! Minions! From now on, I will give you more strength, but if any of you fail me this time, I will put you back where you came from! Now, let's head out!"

*****

"Dark Minions, use the speed I gave you to clear out this office building!"

*****

"It's time. He's at the office building in downtown Saint Louis. One thing, Lord with a Hood—his powers are enhanced. So be careful."

"Okay, I will."

I ran there, but when I was about five blocks away, the Dark Minions noticed. They started to run at me with the speed they were given. I used my electric powers on the concrete, causing it to run down the road at them and knock them out.

When I got to the office, Evil Lord with a Hood had already cleared out the building. He turned around and said, "Ah, Lord with a Hood, you came for the finale! Now let's cut this building." He got out his Dark Sword and swung it sideways.

There was a black effect out of the sword that went through the building cleanly. The building started to fall, and there were people in its path. So I raced over there and used my force powers to hold it in the air. Then I told the people to move away from the area and put it down.

Evil Lord with a Hood then said, "I have the strongest powers."

I said, "It's not about how strong you are. It's where your strength comes from."

"I have strength, and no one has more power than me! Not even you, Lord with a Hood!" Then he ran.

People started coming over to me. One little boy came up to me and asked where my strength came from. I told him, "God, who made everything and loves everyone so much he gave his Son to us. His Son died on a cross and rose so we could rise too."

Then the crowd started to sing "Amazing Grace"!

I went up to one of the building roofs and listened to them sing. After they finished, I went back home and listened to Joy FM radio station.

I rejoiced in the Lord greatly that now at length you have revived your concern for me. You were indeed concerned for me, but you had no opportunity. Not that I am speaking of being in need, for I have learned in whatever situation I am to be content. I know how to be brought low, and I know how to abound. In any and every circumstance, I have learned the secret of facing plenty and hunger, abundance and need. I can do all things through him who strengthens me. (Philippians 4:10–13)

Episode 8

The Grace of God

It had been three days since Evil Lord with a Hood had his powers enhanced and the crowd started singing "Amazing Grace." In the past three days, I was focusing on how much grace he has, because if we're all honest, we will find we have all fallen short, even me. Even now, since I got these powers, I wondered why he chose me. God's grace is greater than we can ever imagine! We all think we have to earn grace, but he already gave it on the cross. We can never earn it, but he gives it to us because he loves us! No matter what you've done or where you go, he will never leave!

*****

"Minions! I told you what would happen if one of you failed me! Now I will show you." *Poof.* "Now, do you want to end up like him?" Evil Lord with a Hood asked. The minions shook their heads, and he said, "Good! Then strategize a better plan!"

One of them came over and showed him.

"Ah, hostages. We haven't tried that yet. This plan will stop Lord with a Hood in his tracks! We're going to Saint Louis Mercy Hospital."

*****

"Hello, people of Mercy Hospital. No one is leaving until I have gotten rid of Lord with a Hood."

"Oh yeah, who's going to stop us?"

"Me! You are brave. You're coming with me. Minions, select random people and leave the rest. He won't be able to resist."

*****

"Lord with a Hood, it is time. Go to Mercy Hospital. He is there. He has hostages. You know what to do."

I went. He was at the top of the building with the hostages. So I ran up the building to get up there.

"Ah, Lord with a Hood, you have beaten me for the last time. My patience has run out! Either you surrender, or this brave man and old woman go splat on the ground! You're not fast enough to save both!"

"I will not surrender. You choose evil instead of hope. I will not surrender to evil. I serve God."

"So be it. Good luck."

"Aaahhh!"

I used my speed to go down the building and grabbed the old woman. Then I used my force powers to stop the speed of the man falling and brought him down slowly.

"No! You will not beat me again!" So I said to him, "I showed you hope, but you chose evil." Then he came at me with his swords, and a power emerged from me in the form of a force field, a part of my force powers that I didn't know I could do.

Evil Lord with a Hood hit it with his sword, but it did not go through. Then he said, "I will get you next time!" and left.

The people came to me and thanked me. The man I saved came over to me and said, "This is a hero."

I said to him, "I am no hero. I came because Jesus came for us. He loves us more than we can imagine. He is the one who gives me strength to help those who need it."

They all gave their gratitude to God.

I went home and thanked God that his grace is far more than we imagine.

> But by the grace of God, I am what I am, and his grace towards me was not in vain. On the contrary, I worked harder than any of them, though it was not I, but the grace of God that is with me. (1 Corinthians 15:10)

Episode 9

Love Is Stronger Than Hate

It had been two weeks since the Mercy Hospital incident. Since then, I had been helping those in need. Sometimes we need to be weak to be strong because only in our weakness do we start to look up. When Jesus suffered, he was weak, but his strength was in giving people hope. He died because of hate, but he conquered death because of love for his people. So I had been showing his kindness for others to look up to.

*****

"You had one job, to find a better plan, and you failed! This is what happens when you fail!" *Poof.* "I'll do it myself! We find him and give him a surprise."

*****

"Lord with a Hood, Evil Lord with a Hood is coming to find you. Be alert."
"Okay, God."

*****

"Let's start with what direction he comes from. When I did something in downtown Saint Louis, he came from the west, but when it was in Saint Charles, he came from the south."

"Ah yes, I know what part of the city he's in. Chesterfield area. He cannot escape us now!"

*****

Later that day, I was helping people who had questions about Jesus's love close to where I live. I said to them, "He loves us more than we can imagine and understand." Then they started praising him.

After that, I started to run back to my house, but then I got hit out of nowhere and saw Evil Lord with a Hood.

"Ah, Lord with a Hood, you think you can beat me and get away with it!"

I said to him, "I don't think about myself but for God's people."

"I don't care what happens as long as I have what I want! I will be better than you because I am not weak like you! No one is going to stand in my way!"

"My strength comes from Jesus, and love is stronger than hate."

He came at me with his swords, but I used my force powers to push him back. He came at me again, and I dodged. Then he said, "Let's see how strong love really is," and he created a black hole above the housing zone not too far from where I live. I used my speed and got everyone a safe distance away from the black hole. This black hole was bigger than the other ones that had been summoned before. Then I heard God's voice say, "Use your force powers to create a force field around the black hole, then shrink the force field until the black hole is gone." I did just that. It got smaller and smaller until it wasn't there.

Then the people came up to me, and one of them asked, "You choose to save us. Why?"

I said to them, "I chose to help because Jesus chose to love, so I choose to do the same. You may think you're not worth helping, but Jesus knows you are. He loves us more than you know."

They started praising God and went to the destruction that the black hole left, helping each other, caring for those who lost everything and giving each other what they had left.

Out of all my experiences of this war, this was the best by far! Seeing those who lost everything still lift each other up—that's what true strength is.

> The steadfast love of the Lord never ceases; his mercies never come to an end; they are new every morning. Great is your faithfulness. The Lord is my portion, says my soul; therefore, I will hope in him. (Lamentations 3:22–24)

Episode 10

God Understands

It had been a week and three days since Evil Lord with a Hood destroyed homes close to where I lived. Since then, I talked to God about his understanding. He said, "I love them more than they know, and I understand that it is hard for them to understand." God does not judge us by our sin but rather by our hearts. God knows there are people who don't understand, but he doesn't hold it against them. It's only when we know him but truly deny him. Jesus came for our hearts. The mind will die with the body, but our heart is our soul. It will live forever if our hearts believe there is hope. So I've been helping people understand, and the way I did this was by confessing my weakness so they knew they were not alone. I also told them I wear black as a symbol to show that I was no better than them. The black represented that I was still a sinner even though I had powers.

*****

"How come we always fail! I want Lord with a Hood rid of! I hate him! He will pay for destroying my plans! Now I'll destroy him! It's time for him to see my full wrath! We are going to Saint Peters to demonstrate my full power! Let's start at Mid Rivers Mall."

*****

27

Poof. "People of the mall, Lord with a Hood made his final mistake! Now destruction is on his hands!" *Poof poof poof poof.* "Hahaha haha!"

*****

"Lord with a Hood, Evil Lord with a Hood is at Mid Rivers Mall."

"Okay, God."

"Before you go, he is very angry at you, so be careful."

I used my speed to get there, and a lot of the interior was destroyed. Then I saw Evil Lord with a Hood, who said, "You got in my way for the final time! Now you will pay!"

Poof. The ceiling started to collapse, and there were two people who were under it. I used my speed and got them out of the way. Then Evil Lord with a Hood came at me with his swords and kicked me into a wall. I got up and ran at him with my swords, but he blocked me. He then made a black hole, so I used my force powers to make a force field around it and started to make it smaller, but then he blasted me with his advanced laser gun.

Then he said, "This all could have been avoided if you stayed out of my way! Now you will die alone."

I saw people behind Evil Lord with a Hood, and then they said, "He's not alone because he showed us we are never alone." Then they started throwing stuff at him.

I said, "They're right, and I can self-heal because God healed me. He is more powerful than you are." Then I used my electric powers, and he went flying into a store in the mall.

The people came over and said, "We may not understand, but we understand he loves us!" They started praising God.

I went to see if Evil Lord with a Hood was still there, but he fled the scene. I went home and thanked God for his understanding.

And Jesus said, "Father, forgive them, for
they know not what they do." And they cast lots
to divide his garments. (Luke 23:34)

Episode 11

The Joy of God

It had been five days since Evil Lord with a Hood's attack on the mall. Since then, I had been helping people find joy. Whether it was paying for someone's items and telling them I did it because he first did it for me, or the big things like helping people rebuild from the destruction Evil Lord with a Hood caused. Having God's joy is the best thing you can ever imagine. His joy is not ours, where we receive something, but it is the joy that he loves us and we know we are his. He loves us more than we can imagine, and when he takes us home, we'll have no pain or sorrow. There will be endless hope and joy. That's what true joy is, not what you have right now, but what we will have.

*****

"I will bring Lord with a Hood to an end! I must kill people's joy so they have no hope! I know just the place people get joy. We're going to Six Flags! Ah, look at the joy at this place just to let it crumble. Ah, the Ferris wheel, a good place to start." *Poof.*

"Aaaaaaaaa!"

"Yes, scream in terror! Hahahaha!"

*****

"Lord with a Hood, it is time. Evil Lord with a Hood is at Six Flags."

"Okay, on it."

I used my speed to get to Six Flags. The Ferris wheel was about to collapse with people still on it. Using my force powers, I brought the wheel down slowly to let each person get off by rolling it.

After everyone was off, Evil Lord with a Hood started clapping and then said, "Good job. I knew you were going to come. Now I'm going to steal your joy! Like you did!"

"You only wanted to be selfish. That's not joy, that's self-pride."

"Well, all I care about now is destroying you!"

He came at me with his swords, so I blocked them with mine. At the same time I blocked them, he kicked me into the sky. I landed on the roof of the roller coaster entrance. Then Evil Lord with a Hood ran up there and punched me through the roof, and I landed in the roller coaster.

Evil Lord with a Hood said, "Now I'll give you joy, then take it away!"

Then the roller coaster started, and I was on it. Then I saw Evil Lord with a Hood had destroyed the track. When I got to the top, the roller coaster started to go down, then fell into the broken track with me inside. It fell straight down, so I was not hurt. I got out of the dust from when it fell.

Evil Lord with a Hood said, "How? No one can survive that!"

I said, "How is not as important as why, because the joy of God gives me strength. Not the joy of man-made things."

"I don't care what gives you strength! All I care about is getting rid of you!"

He came at me again with his swords. I used my force powers, and he went flying all the way over to Hurricane Harbor. I ran over there and saw he landed in the wave pool. He attacked me, so I pushed him with my force powers again, and he landed in Lazy River.

The people came over to me and said, "You showed us that it's not what we do that gives us joy but Jesus." They started praising God, saying, "Jesus is our joy," and then the rest of them said, "Hallelujah!"

I went to see if Evil Lord with a Hood was in Lazy River, but he was nowhere to be found, so I went home.

> Then he said to them, "Go your way. Eat the fat and drink sweet wine and send portions to anyone who has nothing ready, for this day is holy to our Lord. And do not be grieved, for the joy of the Lord is your strength." (Nehemiah 8:10)

Episode 12

God's Faithfulness

It had been three days since the incident at Six Flags. Since then, I had been seeing God's faithfulness. He came down to live like us so we could see how much he loves us. He was beaten, mocked, and hung on a cross. He loved them even though they killed him because, deep down inside, he saw they were hurting but wanted hope. So, he died and rose to give us hope. He forgives because he sees what we do not. He is faithful to us who don't understand and know his love.

*****

"I hate Lord with a Hood! I don't care what God has to offer because I have everything at my fingertips! Lord with a Hood has faith in God? Then I'll try to turn their faith to me! We're heading to Alton to show how faithful I can be. Hahahaha! Minions cause havoc on the city!"

They nodded and started destroying things.

"Ah yes. Bring them to their knees to me! Ah, you come to ask for my help."

"We know who you are and represent. You can do what you want, but we will not worship you. We worship God who sent Lord with a Hood to help!"

"So be it! Maybe you'll think twice! Bring them to the river! I'll make them an example!"

*****

"Lord with a Hood, he's in Alton."

"Okay, I'll go."

I used my speed to run there, and I saw Evil Lord with a Hood with three people by the river.

Evil Lord with a Hood then said, "Lord with a Hood, since they decided God over me, they will now drown!"

He pushed them in the river, so I used my speed on the water and used my force powers to pull them out, then sat them on the shore of the river. After I got the last one out, I started running back up the river. But before I got back, I saw Evil Lord with a Hood run up the river at me. I got hit and fell under the water.

Then I heard God's voice say, "Create a force field," so I did. The water was outside the force field, like I was in a bubble. I got above the water with the force field.

Evil Lord with a Hood said, "You should have drowned!"

I said to him, "God is faithful to those who believe."

"You know what! I really hate you! Why can't I get rid of you! If I can't get rid of you, the black hole will!"

He created a black hole, and it pulled me in. It was dark with no light or anything. Then I heard God's voice say, "Alexander, use your strongest weapon—your faith."

I cried out, "GOD, MY TRUST IS IN YOU!" Then I saw outside the black hole and walked out.

Evil Lord with a Hood then said, "No one ever can escape a black hole! There's no way you can just walk out!"

"I told you before—with God, all things are possible! Your hate clouds your perspective."

"I don't care what your God can do! all I care about is what I want!"

He slashed at me with his swords. I used my force powers, blasting him across the river.

The people came to me and said, "Thank Jesus for his faithfulness," and then brought a speaker out. They started singing together, praising God.

I ran home thanking God for how faithful he is.

> No temptation has overtaken you that is not common to man. God is faithful, and he will not let you be tempted beyond your ability, but with the temptation he will also provide the way of escape, that you may be able to endure it. (1 Corinthians 10:13)

Episode 13

Praise God

It had been four days since the incident in Alton with Evil Lord with a Hood. In certain situations, praise is the only way to defeat the lies because when we know who he is, and the lies come, and we praise him for what he has done, then the walls of lies fall at the sound of our praise. Seeing his love toward us is always enough to praise because his love is nothing that we have known in this world and understands all. He is the God of love, and he never leaves the ones who have hope behind. He gave everything for us, we can't earn it by ourselves, but our hearts are worth more to him. We praise because of how much he loves us.

*****

"I want Lord with a Hood out of my way! Ah, I got an idea! If I can create a black hole, I can create multiple of them! He can't stop all of them! Minions, prepare! We are going to bring Ballwin to its knees!"

*****

"People of Ballwin, you will follow me, or this city will crumble!"

"We will not follow you, for you stand with evil. We know what Lord with a Hood taught us about the love of God. You may destroy all we have, but we have all in the name of Jesus!"

"So be it!"

*****

"Lord with a Hood, he's in Ballwin, and he is planning to create multiple black holes."

"Okay, on it!"

I used my speed, and I saw Evil Lord with a Hood on the top of a building with twenty-five dark minions.

He said, "Lord with a Hood, you have destroyed my plans for the final time! Now you will see the destruction of Ballwin!"

Then I said, "You have destroyed them by hate. Now his love for his people is what will bring you down."

"Catch me if you can!"

Evil Lord with a Hood used his speed and ran, creating black holes while doing so. I ran after him, closing them with my force powers. After the eighth one he made, and he realized had I closed them all.

He said, "How did you close them so fast? Never mind! I don't care you destroyed all my plans. You will be destroyed. Minions, attack!"

They all came after me. I got out my swords and ran at them. I slashed ten of them, but the eleventh one cut me on my right arm with its sword. I used my electric powers to get rid of the rest. Then they all turned to ash.

The people came to me, and one said, "Let me help with that wound."

Then I said, "You do not know I can self-heal, and that's okay. There's much we still will not understand about the power of God. So let me show you." I used my left hand to touch my right arm and used my healing powers.

Then they said "We do not understand the power of God, but we know how much he loves us. That's enough to praise him." So they started praising God for his love for them.

I left and went home to praise God.

> With joy you will draw water from the wells of salvation. And you will say in that day, "Give thanks to the Lord, call upon his name, make known his deeds among the peoples, proclaim that his name is exalted. Sing praises to the Lord, for he has done gloriously; let this be made known in all the earth." (Isaiah 12:3–5)

Episode 14

Who Can Stand Against God?

It had been four days since the attack on Ballwin. Since then, I had been teaching people the power of God. Not by mine but by showing them that he created the whole earth, because if he created all the earth and knows everyone's name, then that is proof of his power. Another thing is that Jesus conquered death, which no one can defeat. That's the true power of God. He conquered death so that one day, we will be with him. That's the true power of love that makes the enemy run. That's the true power of God—his love for us.

*****

"I want Lord with a Hood gone! He's destroyed my plans numerous times! Now I want him rid of! We're going to end him at Florissant! This time, I'm taking forty-five minions. He will not defeat me this time!"

*****

"People of Florissant, since I already know you will not follow, I will raid your city until you will surrender! Dark Minions, raid this city! I will destroy it with my black holes! I was prepared, and now Lord With a Hood will be too late!"

*****

"Lord with a Hood, he has started his attack already in Florissant."

"Okay, I'm on it."

I ran there. When I got there, I saw the minions trashing the city and black holes starting to destroy it. Then I heard God's voice say, "Go for the black holes."

I ran through the city, closing all of them with my force powers. After I closed the last one, I got slammed into a wall by Evil Lord with a Hood.

Then he said, "Last time, you destroyed my plans. Now I will destroy you!" He pulled me off the wall and slammed me into a window of a store repeatedly. Then he got out his sword and said, "You made your last mistake! Now you will die!"

I was badly hurt, so I used my force powers and pushed him through the roof of the store and healed myself. Then I saw the minions still trashing the city. I ran through the city, clearing out the minions.

After I was finished with the minions, the people came to me. One of them said, "Who can stand against the power of our God, for his love is stronger!" Then they started to thank God and praise him.

I went home and said, "Thank you, for your love is unimaginable for Satan to stand against."

> What then shall we say to these things? If
> God is for us, who can be against us? He who did
> not spare his own son but gave him up for us all,
> how will he not also with him graciously give us
> all things? (Romans 8:31–32)

God Is with Us

It had been two days since the attack on Florissant. Since then, I had been spreading the news that God is with us. It may not seem like he is, but he is closer than we see because he is within us. Sometimes we want to be cured or fixed, but only in the fire, flood, and the storm can we see it's not about being at our best because only at our worst do we start to see clearly. Jesus used people you would not expect. He didn't choose people who were strong but rather whom we could call weak. But he does not see it as weakness. Only when we look up are we strong because our weakness leads to him. He is the God of love, and he is with us.

"I want Lord with a Hood dead! He has destroyed my plans! Now my wrath will be toward him to die! Minions! Prepare sixty Dark Minions and head for Des Peres!"

*****

"People of Des Peres, we know you will not surrender to me! You then will surrender to destruction! Minions! Do what must be done to get them to surrender!"

*****

"Lord with a Hood, Evil Lord with a Hood's in Des Peres."

"Okay, on it."

I ran there and saw Evil Lord with a Hood leading an attack. The Dark Minions in that neighborhood were pulling people out of their houses and holding their swords up to them. Using my speed, I then slashed all twenty of them with my swords, and they turned to ash.

Evil Lord with a Hood then said, "You have destroyed my plans—now you will die!"

He ran at me with his advanced laser gun and shot a building. It started to fall on me, so I used my force powers to create a force field around me. Then I saw Evil Lord with a Hood create a black hole above me and start to pull me in with the debris from the building. I used my speed to run on the debris and used my force powers to push Evil Lord with a Hood back.

He then said, "Minions, destroy him!"

I used my electric powers on the remaining forty and made a chain reaction. Then they turned to ash, and Evil Lord with a Hood ran at me with his swords. It cut my left side.

Evil Lord with a Hood then said, "You could have stayed out of my way, and you wouldn't have to die! Now you will!"

Then the people came up to him, and one of them said, "God is with us!" The people started throwing stuff at him.

He started to walk over to them with his swords. I healed myself, and he raised his sword at them. I came beside him and used my force powers. He then went flying over a house.

The people then came to me. One of them said, "We know who you stand for. Since you showed us he is always with us, we came to help no matter what would happen to us." Then they started praising God, and I left to go home.

> I bless the Lord who gives me counsel; in
> the night also my heart instructs me. I have set
> the Lord always before me; because he is at my
> right hand, I shall not be shaken. Therefore, my
> heart is glad, and my whole being rejoices; my
> flesh also dwells secure. (Psalm 16:7–9)

God Is Greater Than Hate

It had been three days since Evil Lord with a Hood's attack on Des Peres. Since then, I wondered when this war would be over. I turned to God for answers. Then I heard God's voice say, "This one is coming to an end, but another will arise."

Then I said to God, "Your love is greater than the power of hate. I will follow you to the end." Sometimes, we think we have to be something more, but Jesus is love. We were not made to judge the world but to show it hope. Sometimes we must get off the mountain to get to others' level like he first did for us. There is no greater love than God's, the one that makes the blind see and the deaf hear. The one who calms the sea and walks on it. The one who commands the dead to live again and who rose from the grave to conquer death for the love of his people. There is no God greater who can offer this much love. For he is the God of love and created all.

*****

"I want Lord with a Hood dead! He has destroyed my plans for the final time! We are going to war! Head for the city of Clayton with one hundred Dark Minions! Lord with a Hood made his final mistake!"

*****

"People of Clayton, I know what you have chosen. Now war is coming!"

*****

"Lord with a Hood, Evil Lord with a Hood has started his attack. Head for the city of Clayton."

"Okay, on it!"

I ran using my speed, and I saw the biggest black hole that he had made. It was starting to tear the towers. Part of the tower started to fall, and under that area was a crowd of people. I used my force powers to create a force field around the people. When the debris fell down, it hit the force field, but the force field shielded them. I used my force powers again and put a force field around the black hole, then made it smaller and smaller until it was nothing. I then saw Evil Lord with a Hood with a hundred Dark Minions.

He said, "You have destroyed my plans for the final time! Now you will die!"

He ran at me then kicked me through the window of a tower. I got up, and he ran at me again. I used my force powers, pushing him back.

Then he said, "Twenty minions, surround Lord with a Hood!"

They surrounded me, and Evil Lord with a Hood started to run at me. I used my electric powers to cause a chain reaction. Twenty of his minions turned to ash, and he was flung back through a window with my electricity.

He got up and said, "Dark Minions, destroy Lord with a Hood." He then ran off, shooting his advanced laser gun on random buildings.

The eighty Dark Minions that were left put up their swords and ran at me. I used my force powers on the ground, stomping and knocking forty of them down. The other forty ran at me. I used my electric powers, and they turned to ash. The other forty got up and ran at me. I then used my swords and ran at them with my speed. They all turned to ash. I ran after Evil Lord with a Hood with my speed. He was using his advanced laser gun, so I used my force powers to push him, and he went into a wall.

Then he said "Think fast" and shot a building with people under it. I ran over there and created another force field to protect them. Then Evil Lord with a Hood said, "War is coming, and you will be the first to fall!" Then he ran off.

The people then came over to me. One of them then said, "Thank God for he is greater!" They then started thanking and praising God. So I went home and did the same and prepared for war.

> This is my commandment, that you love one another as I have loved you. Greater love has no one than this, that someone lay down his life for his friends. You are my friends if you do what I command you. No longer do I call you servants, for the servant does not know what his master is doing, but I have called you friends, for all that I have heard from my Father I have made known to you. You did not choose me, but I chose you and appointed you that you should go and bear fruit and that your fruit should abide, so that whatever you ask the Father in my name, he may give it to you. These things I command you, so that you will love one another. (John 15:12–17)

Episode 17

The Battle Belongs to You

It was a day since the attack on Clayton. Since then, I have asked God how I will know when the war will be won. He told me I would know when the time came. I said to him, "The battle belongs to you. For I do not know when it will be won, but I lift my eyes to the one who knows." Sometimes we fight each other, but our battle is not with each other but to fight for hope. We all have fallen short. So why do we try to be better? He chose the weak to lead the strong because they knew they were not worthy. The Pharisees thought they could keep the commandments, but the truth is, you can't keep it. That's why Jesus came to give hope, which he has sealed in our hearts. We may say we don't want him from our mind, but what does our heart look for? We see the world has fallen, but what would we see if we look past the outside and into the heart of God's people? Would we see sin, or would we see a person who wants hope? His greatest commandment is love, and the battle belongs to him.

*****

"Dark Minions, the time has come for our attack on Saint Louis! They will fall to my power, and Lord with a Hood will be no more! March to downtown Saint Louis! We'll start at the front of the river in front of the arch! Dark Minions, head to the highways and cut them off! I'll start here at Stan Musial Veterans Memorial Bridge!"

****

"Lord with a Hood, he has started his attack on downtown Saint Louis."

"Okay, on it."

I ran there with my speed and saw Evil Lord with a Hood with his advanced laser gun shooting at the poles that kept it up. There were cars driving up and down it still. So I used my force field to block one side, then when the other cars were through, I put it on the other side. Then I repeated the process for the opposite side. I saw Evil Lord with a Hood walk toward me and say, "The final battle has begun, and you will be the one to fall!"

Then I said to him, "It's not my battle, and I know how it ends. I will not be the one to fall because I stand with the strong foundation of love."

"Let's test that then!" He ran at me so I used my force powers, and he went flying to the arch. So I ran to the arch. Then he said, "Now I'll destroy the gateway to the west with my black hole! Also, my whole army of Dark Minions are at every highway entering Saint Louis! Choose wisely. You can't protect both! Hahahaha!"

> And that all this assembly may know that the Lord saves not with sword and spear. For the battle is the Lord's, and he will give you into our hand. When the Philistine arose and came and drew near to meet David, David ran quickly toward the battle line to meet the Philistine. And David put his hand in his bag and took out a stone and slung it and struck the Philistine on his forehead. The stone sank into his forehead, and he fell on his face to the ground. (1 Samuel 17:47–49)

Episode 18

Against All Odds

Against all odds, what seemed impossible was not. He never leaves someone defenseless in the battle. Right now, it may seem like a no-win situation, but he had already won, and he was with me. Evil Lord with a Hood may seem to have the upper hand, but he did not because God has never failed me now, and he will never fail.

I heard God's voice say, "Close the black hole, and then deal with the Dark Minions." So I used my force field around the black hole and closed it, but part of the black hole took a bit of the steel off the top if the arch. It started to split at the top with the people still up there. I used my force powers to hold it together, and it stopped.

Then Evil Lord with a Hood said, "You may have stopped the destruction of the arch, but you don't have time to protect the highways! Hahahaha!"

I ran to Highway 44 first. When I got there, I realized they had a bomb and were planning to blow up the highway. I grabbed the bomb and used my electric powers to get rid of the minions. I did the same for Highways 64 and 70 too. After I grabbed the bombs, I realized they were going to detonate in thirty seconds. I used my speed and ran to the Mississippi River, throwing the bombs in.

I saw Evil Lord with a Hood. He said, "I hate you! You will die by my power! You have destroyed all my plans! Now I'll destroy you myself! I will be more powerful than you and your God! Now see the true power of evil!" He ran at me, raising his sword, and black holes started forming all over the city. I used my force powers, and he went flying. I ran to where he fell, but I saw a red speed trail. I knew it was him, so I ran after him.

> Then the disciples came to Jesus privately and said, "Why could we not cast it out?" He said to them, "Because of your little faith. For truly, I say to you, if you have faith like a grain of mustard seed, you will say to this mountain, 'Move from here to there,' and it will move, and nothing will be impossible for you." (Matthew 17:19–21)

Episode 19

Hope Wins for God's People

If I was being honest, I could have never come all this way on my own. When I was younger, I was weak, but God did not see it that way. My friends saw I stood with God and left. God picked me up and said I was not alone. I saw myself as weak, but when I looked up, I started seeing how he did. Sometimes we are brought down, but our weakness is what helps others. Only then do we see through him.

Since I was sixteen, I was always talking about him until I was twenty-four—that's when I became Lord with a Hood. My weakness is my greatest strength because only then do we see it his way. I ran by McKinley Bridge in a district warehouse area. I saw him go into a warehouse, so I followed him in. Then the lights in the warehouse came on. There I saw the advanced laser gun he used, a bag of money, and a computer pinpointing where he had attacked.

He then said, "This is my lair! Now this is the finale! You will be the one to die. though!"

Then he turned on the computer and showed me the city. In the city, the black holes were getting bigger. Evil Lord with a Hood said, "You and your city will fall!"

Then I said to him, "You have chosen evil, and evil will fall with God's love."

"So be it! Now you will die!"

He ran at me with his swords, and I blocked them with mine. Then he kicked me, and I landed on the second floor of the warehouse. He ran up, so I used my force powers, and he went flying, hitting a generator in the warehouse. He ran at me again with his swords, so I used my electric powers, stomping the ground, and the electricity ran up the floor at him, but he dodged it. It hit the generator, causing it to explode, and we both went flying. The building caught on fire.

Evil Lord with a Hood then ran at me again. I heard God's voice say, "Destroy his swords, and the black holes will be closed." So I ran at him, putting my hope in God that when I hit the swords, they would break. I blocked his swords, and they started to crack. Then he kicked me, and I hit the wall. I got up and used my electric powers on the swords, running at him. The swords crumbled with the electricity, and I struck him with my sword on his left side.

Then he said, "I hate you," and fell to the ground.

I left, heading home, and prayed to God. I thanked him for all he had done when I was weak. I turned on the television, and Fox 2 News was on. They came to people and asked "How do you think Lord with a Hood defeated the impossible?"

They all said, "Lord with a Hood stands with God, and with God nothing is impossible!"

"There we have it—the city's protector that was sent by God! Lord with a Hood!"

> To the Jews I became as a Jew, in order to win Jews. To those under the law I became as one under the law, though not being myself under the law, that I might win those under the law. To those outside the law I became as one outside the law, not being outside the law of God but under the law of Christ, that I might win those outside the law. To the weak I became weak, that I might win the weak. I have become all things to all people, that by all means I might save some. I do it all for the sake of the gospel, that I may share with them in its blessings. (1 Corinthians 9:20–23)

A fiction story but a true God.

About the Author

Arthur Steers lives in O'Fallon, Missouri, and has a heart for Jesus in creative concepts. In elementary school, the character Lord with a Hood came to him and stuck. At that time, he did not understand who God was until after his brother died. After that, he started to understand more about God's hope, grace, and love, but still not that well. When his grandma died, he felt like he lost everything, but in the midst of that, Jesus was there, reminding him to mourn for those who are here rather than the ones with God. He now stands in the hope, grace, and love of Jesus. Arthur is working on multiple books based on Lord with a Hood and other characters.